The
LOST MARBLE
NOTEBOOK

of

FORGOTTEN GIRL
&
RANDOM BOY

The
LOST MARBLE NOTEBOOK
of
FORGOTTEN GIRL & RANDOM BOY

Marie Jaskulka

Sky Pony Press
New York

Sky Pony Press books may be purchased in bulk at special discounts for sales promotion, corporate gifts, fund-raising, or educational purposes. Special editions can also be created to specifications. For details, contact the Special Sales Department, Sky Pony Press, 307 West 36th Street, 11th Floor, New York, NY 10018 or info@skyhorsepublishing.com.

Sky Pony® is a registered trademark of Skyhorse Publishing, Inc.®, a Delaware corporation.

Visit our website at www.skyponypress.com.

10 9 8 7 6 5 4 3 2 1

Library of Congress Cataloging-in-Publication Data is available on file.

Cover design by Rain Saukas

Print ISBN: 978-1-63220-426-4
Ebook ISBN: 978-1-63450-004-3

Printed in the United States of America

to Jane, who can tell me anything
and Mom, who always listens

Black Fate

They fight
like two rabid rivals,
forgetting
they spawned
an innocent bystander
who listens
to every word.

Most kids
wish their parents
were still together—
not me.

She screams, "You
bastard! How could you
do this
to us?"

Dad answers in
silence, which
Mom pierces
with
curses
until Dad shuts her up
with his big man voice,

"Because I can't
stand this anymore—
I can't stand you and . . ."

. . . = Me?
I am above it all,
literally,

in a pink bedroom
that doesn't fit me anymore.

Books lie
open and closed—
millions of
happily ever afters
surround me.

Desperate for air,
I go to the window.

With my rose-colored curtains
split wide open,
I check the neighborhood
spread out before me
like Legos. I am imagining
jumping—maybe
that would shut them up—
when
I spot a Random Boy,
clad in black,
walking my street,
focused and sinister,
smoke rising from him
as though he's on fire.

He doesn't know I exist
until
I thrust open the window
and lean out into the cold.

I don't know why, but I
stick two fingers in my mouth
and whistle.

Everything about me goes rigid
as he turns his head
toward me
and listens—
not to me,
but to them.

"Godammit!" Mom screams.
"That is mine!"

Whatever it is
shatters
as the boy
smiles pitifully
and waves.

I wave, too,
and watch him
approach.
His eyes don't leave mine.

When he gets to
the sidewalk
in front of me, he
watches me
for a second,
listening to my parents'
love
self-destructing,
and his smile changes.

His eyes trail down
the façade of my house, conspiring.
I can feel my world shifting as
he climbs up

onto the porch roof
adeptly
while my father screams,
unaware.

He is at my window
asking, *"Rough day?"*
as though he does this
sort of thing
all the time.

He gets comfortable
on the sill.

He is older than me,
but just as—I don't know.
He offers me a cigarette,
which I take.

I don't usually
take things from strangers,
or smoke,
and boys don't usually
try to save me
either.

But I take the cigarette
and the light he offers
and my first drag of
nicotine relief
because

I can just tell
this random moment
is going to change me
forever.

Window

He stays
and speaks loudest
over the parts
that are hardest to hear
as though he's heard it all before.

He doesn't even flinch.

"Are they always like this?" he asks.

I nod.

*"Are you always
so beautiful?"*

I blush. I cough. I drop my cigarette,
and we both watch it flicker and spin
to the ground.

"Want to get out of here?"

I look down
and envision myself
careening
toward
the
pavement.

"I won't let you fall."

Before I can answer,
the door below us
bursts open.
Out flies my father.

Together, this stranger and I watch
the man in my life
desert me
without
a backward glance.

Relief

When Dad disappears,
he doesn't take the time
to tell me good-bye;
I guess he thought it was implied.

He just gets in his car
and blows away
this town
and me.

Mom's in audible tears.
Only this Random Boy
remembers I exist,
watching me
more closely
than I've ever been seen.
I am too torn up
by the goings on
inside
to hide,
so I don't know what he sees.

"Come with me," he says.

He nods
down a darkened street below,
where lonely kids meet to waste
their time together.

I've always avoided the
group on the stoop
who loiter and litter and leer
when people walk by.

I've been too busy
trying to evade
my parents' crimes
to commit my own.

Hollow,
I climb down
from my childhood
room.

I bloom.

He leads.
And I follow.

Meet the Kids

That's when I start hanging
at the corner
with boys
whose hair is too long
to have parents who care.

Did my mother care?
Hard to tell with all her self-
pity in the way.

That's when I start smoking,
because the smell matches
how my heart feels.

And my Random Boy
doesn't ditch me.
Rather,
after he introduces me,
he backs away.
I figured he'd try to seduce me,
but instead he studies me from afar
like I am the only thing
in his sight
that isn't transparent.

When the two of us occupy the same space,
the ground shakes
from the pressure.
Bystanders feel it, too.

"Oh girl," some chick named Mary says,
"you are in deep shit."

"How so?" I pushed.

"Bitches been all over that whore
since as long as I can remember,
but I've never seen him stare
a hole through any chick
before."

Trying not to feel excited,
I turn my eyes his way,
after one last look.

At eye contact impact,
the gravitational pull
I felt
toward him
freaked me out, so

I stared him down
until he looked away.

Autobiography

People wonder why I sneer all the time,
why I can't let a mistake go by
without a snide comment,
why I am
such
a
bitch.

Truth is . . .
I'm sick,
physically sick
at the amount of
assholery
in the world
as well as
all the dumbasses who are oblivious to it.

And There's Something Else You Should Know

Mary is determined
to connect.

"You know Noelle?"

"No."

"You know Autumn?"

"No."

"You know Ali?"

"No."

"You know . . .
anyone?"

"No"
doesn't satisfy her,
so I say:

"I don't have any
girl friends.
I used to have
a friend named
Sam. We used to play
in mud-pie, glee-filled
backyards. Then
she moved to some
faraway town;
I don't
even remember
the name."

She's one of my more than 2000 friends
on Facebook.

You'd think I'd
have made another
real-life
girl friend
by the age of 15,
but I haven't met
anyone I like
enough to
change.

Making friends
just so I can lose them
is lame.

Mom's "Wise" Words (At Least She's Talking)

"Don't be like me," she says,
which is not what a parent
should say to her child.

"Don't trust anyone, and for
God's sake, honey, don't
fall in love. It will trick you,

chew you up, and then
throw you up all over
the ground. End of story."

Boys

This isn't the first time Dad's left.
He did it last year, too.

That time, I was open
to opening up
about it.

I was camping with
all the kids and—I don't even
know why I did this—
but I let Brian Kipley
go up my shirt.

I never told anyone
that he squeezed my breasts
so hard they ached
for two days after. That he
kept tinkling his fingers
downward even after I
stopped him about 50 times.

I never told anyone
because I was crying
the whole time, and I
guessed he thought he was
doing me
a favor, like
therapy or something.

But it didn't do any good
'cause he told everyone.

Meanwhile

*I don't think
she sees me
watching her*

*as the breeze
catches her curls
in its waggling wind fingers,
and a smile rearranges
her face.*

*But,
when I watch her—
as I do now
as she sways
to keep straight
on the spinning merry-go-round—*

*my heart beats faster than is healthy
as my blood
races down down down . . .*

*My memories drain
to make room
in my head
for only her.*

Get This

My mom found a poem I wrote
called,
"I Hate You So Much It's Love Again."

It was about her.

She said,
"How can you talk about hating me
so much
you want to run away?"

"But you missed the point," I tell her.
"It's love again."

She holds the paper
(stolen from the floor of my bedroom)
as though she has the right
and reads aloud:

"You are a sorry excuse for a mother,
a woman,
to let a man
ruin you."

She explores my face;
she doesn't recognize me
inside these true, callous words.
That much is clear in her blurry eyes.

The older I get,
the more I see
she doesn't really know me
at all,
just some kid
I can't remember being.

I snatch the rogue poem
from her trembling fingers,
crush those words literally, symbolically,
and toss them onto the overflowing trash bin.

She watches, but doesn't
wipe her tears away.
She says, "You have no idea
how hard it is
to lose your heart,
and I hope you never do."

I want to say,
Didn't I lose him, too?

But before I do,
she retreats
to her
bedroom/cave
and shuts out
the world,

including me.

Getting to Know All About Us

"What year are you?"

"Sophomore."

"Got a boyfriend?"

"Why?"
Like I'm going to tell him I've never had a boyfriend.

"So I know who I got to beat up."

"Where do you go?"
I turn the tables.

"I'm not in school.
Graduated in June.
Taking a year off
before . . ."

"Before?"

(shrugs)

"College?"

"Naaaah, not my style."

"Job?"

"Girl, loving you takes up ALL my time."

I blush, despite myself—
and yes, he notices.

Confessing

Mary has her hair
in pig (how appropriate) tails
and her school skirt
rolled
so her hem
is way more than
two inches
above
her knee.

I swear to God.
Catholic girls are
hella slutty.

Don't be a slut-shamer,
I tell myself.
But sometimes it's hard
not to take another girl's
promiscuity
personally.
The sudden competition
sprung
from someone who
a minute ago
was a friend.

Me, I've got on
a plain white T
and too-tight jeans
that cut into my
belly when I sit. I also

don the
requisite
hoodie to
hide
the heart
I wear
on my sleeve.

Mary bends
over without
bending her knees
—ugh—
and when I turn
to see what Random Boy
thinks of all this
teenage waste-
land,
I find him staring
at me.

He nods me closer
and I go to his side.

"Is she for real?"

"You're not enjoying her show?"

"I don't get slapstick."

"No?"

He leans in so I can smell him;
he is
minty tobacco fresh.

"I prefer your exes and ohs
to that ho's
any day."

My grin is involuntary,
my gasp,
audible.

I admit it.
I am smitten as a kitten
with that
Random Boy.

Playing Cool

These days,
it's hard
to keep up
with the changing
styles. They trend
too fast,
peak and fade
before I know
they exist.

It's hard
to have a permanent
heart
in a disposable
world.

So when he leans toward me,
I lean away.

When he tells me I'm beautiful,
I make an ugly face
and snort.

But when he weaves his way
into my daydreams,
I let the thought of him
caress my mind.

I don't admit it to myself
or to him,
but I let those thoughts of him in.

Getting Ready

First, I draw a ballpoint blue
tattoo under my belly button—
not that he's going to see it. But I

carefully let the smallest
bit show. Then, I spray the orchid
perfume he complimented one time.

I'd be lying if I said
I didn't think about him
while painting black lines around my eyes.

I'd be fooling only myself
if I thought these tight jeans
were a sign of my independence.

This two-hour artistic
exhibition is all for him.

Ugh.

Standing Up

Imagine the length
of my letdown
when I get to the place
we meet, flirt, and wonder
to find him absent—
?

Guess I shouldn't expect
him here waiting,
panting
like a puppy,
like he has been,
but I did,
and now I'm chain-smoking,
ignoring everybody's questions,
and searching the
crossroad horizons
for his shape
approaching.

Only he doesn't appear
until more than an hour past
usual, and he's slurring
his steps. Good thing
he's got that tall glass
of water to lean on.
That's the only
reason he's hanging
on to her, right?

Yeah.
Right.

You Can't Live With Them

Why do you look at me one day
and someone else the next?

I saw what you wrote in the
back of her social studies

notebook. Everyone did,
and now I don't believe

a word you say,
said,
will ever utter again.

What Do You Want Me to Do?

Here's my take
on girls—

They are
running a race, and guys
are just hurdles,
one of the ways
they

keep score.

I stare.
I prod.
I beg
with my eyes,
and she denies
every time.

So what do I do? Lie
back and let her heels
dig into my Play-Doh heart? Beg
her for hellos like she
says she wants
or
disregard her like she
does me?

Now, here's the truth
about guys—

It's not about love.
It's about eating,
sleeping,
and sex.

I know
it's douchebaggy,
but it's true.
It FEELS true.

So what do I do?
Give up? Give in?
Deny myself?

Or

navigate
the minefield of
you,
armed
with fronted indifference?

Typical Conversation

"Ever wish your parents were dead?"

"Sometimes."

"I'll kill 'em for you.
All ya have to do is ask."

"You'd have to find my dad first."

"I would. Wouldn't stop
'til I did
if that's what you wanted."

What a weird
thing to say—
romantic, sure,
but weird.
"Like in that movie?"

"What movie?"

"The one
with the girl and the boy
who are neighbors
who get each other
and fall in love
and run away."

He just stares,
smiles.

That Poem

where she reveals
she has secret
wet dreams
starring
his lean
libido.

"That Poem" is
a love letter
to him:

Notice it isn't a like-letter,
a friend request,
a note,

but an "I can't
keep my head
straight
or
off of you"

admission.

Boy,
I feel dirty
just thinking
about you
whether I'm naked
or clothed. I
engage in
you-themed
meditation
to get clean.

Seeing Things

My mom,
lying in her musty covers,
likes to say
she'll get her shit together
someday.

Maybe so.
She is still pretty
beautiful—for a mom.
I notice dudes checking her out
regularly. You know how guys are.

She doesn't pay any mind,
and I don't blame her.
Being that most humans
are liars, or liars in training,
it's the smart thing to do.

On school days,
I get up before the sun,
eat breakfast alone,
and think
maybe this morning
will be the one
when
she starts
over.

Before I leave,
I lean my head
on her closed door.

"Mom."

"Yeah?"

"I'm going."

"Okay."

I wait a few seconds
until she begins
to cry.
Then
I leave.

Typical Conversation, Part 2

"How come you won't look at me?"

"What's the point?"

"Connections."

"What's the point?"

"Love."

(Both of us stare at the cars going by
in opposite directions,
crisscrossing for a nanosecond,
then separating. To be honest,
my heart is beating a million
beats per minute.)

"I write poetry, too, you know."
(I don't believe him. I still don't look at him.)
"I've never told anyone that.
Well, my mom knows."
(Silence.)
"But even she hasn't read it."

(Inhale. Exhale. *Inhale.*
Exhale. Our cigarettes
have a hectic conversation.

Inhale, *Exhale*—

No one else is here
to drown them out.)

"You want to read my poetry sometime?" he asks, and
the air around me sounds like drum rolls and cymbals crashing;
a veritable symphony of swooning resounds,

but all I say is, "Sure."

Dance

If I let you
read mine,
will you let me
read yours?

Obey

He pulls
my hand behind him
so I have no choice
but to follow.

He pulls me down
a side street, glancing
all over, all the time
for bullets
to dodge—
as if this street is some kind of
war zone.

His house
is the same as
all the other houses
on the outside:
white siding,
black shutters.
I am visualizing
the inside
when he tells me—
"Wait here."
—and enters through
a back door
without
me. I twiddle
my fingers
and wallow
because
he doesn't want me

to meet
his family and vice
versa.

He emerges from a
front door with an
echo
of a woman's voice
urging him
to come back,
but he ignores her and
smiles/walks to me—
downward-spiral
notebook in hand.

I follow him farther
down the street
to the periphery woods
that surround the playground, where
we don't play
around.

We climb
into a
dilapidated tree house
decorated with sun-faded, water-bubbly *Playboy*
centerfolds our dads probably
gawped in the '80s.

"What is this place?" I ask.

(I kick a pile of
dry leaves and cigarette butts,
which soften every corner
of this makeshift Shangri-La.)

"*Where I go*
when I don't know
where else to go,"
he explains.

"Charming."

"*Private.*"

He sits in crispy leaves,
and gives his ink-stained book
to
me.

Reading His Words

is
I guess
like
reading
his
diary,
seeing his room,
stealing his heart,
because I read
every genre
of writing
and his—

How can I describe it?

It's like he's cracked open the solid
watermelon
of his heart
and sweet, sticky truth is spilling everywhere.

Fangirl

I asked him
if I could have
a copy of that
one about me
on the
merry-go-round.

He ripped
the original
from his
notebook, and
I glued it in here.

I said,
"I want some others, too,
—to put in my marble notebook—

I want our poems to tell
the story of us."

"My notebook is your notebook," he said.

"Are you sure
you don't want to keep them?"

He just
pointed
to his head
and then
to his heart.

This Is Getting Ridiculous

Grounded
because
I nitpicked
about
the state of her:
I said,
"Why don't you
get up and
get a job
and get a life?"

And she called
me a bitch,
a grounded bitch.

I know we fight a lot.
We stab sharp word arrows
through each other's hearts
daily so I should be used to it,

but the first time your mother
calls you the b-word,
you feel
the sting
straight
down
to
your
toes.

Man

Usually,
all I see
is her
and the hazy halo
the headlights
and rain make
around her face,
the starry
glimmer
in her dark eyes.

Usually, she is
as easy to spot
as a full moon
late at night.

She said she'd show.

But tonight
the sky is black,
moonless,
and all the girls
who pretend
to
love her
bump against me
and
betray her
trust.

It's a devastating thing,
the teen age.

Lust is . . .
when all the someones

who wouldn't talk to me
the night before
spontaneously
combust into
whores.

Missed Opportunist

Let me show you
how it goes:

He's all,
I love you
love you
You,
You,
Just YOU,
and she's all
but wait,
and then she
slowly
gives
herself
over,

just as
he sleeps
with
someone else
while
she
keeps
her lovelight burning
like
a dumbass.

It's Like This

One minute you're hot
(okay, you're always hot),
and then
you cut like a car chase
so fast I can't
follow.

So I deal
by drowning
my thoughts of you
in an alcohol
sea, and I become
this other me,
who doesn't care,
or think,
or understand.

Just drink drink drink
and screw screw screw
things up.

To Get Back at Him

I give him the silent treatment,
only
in eye contact.

I go to the place
where the boys congregate
and I make sure I look good—

just like before,
but different now,
meaner somehow.

I hang on Greg's
every word, and I
laugh at his asinine
jokes, and I'm not
going to lie,

I watch the frown
lines deepen
like scars
into that
Random Boy's
face,

and I
enjoy it.

Intimate Conversation between Two People in the Middle of a Crowd

"I don't like when you're mad at me."

"Too bad."

"What do I have to do?"

"Go back in time and change history."

"How far?"

"Huh?"

"I'm not a virgin, you know. I'm a guy."

"What's that supposed to mean?"

"Sex isn't that important to guys. It's like breathing. I don't even realize I'm doing it."

"Well, that's really sad." (I light a cigarette
whenever something pisses me off. That's why
I smoke so many cigarettes.)

"What's sad about it?"

"It's not like when we were little
and everything was magic.
Now, it seems like so few things
in this life are awesome.
The truest moments are scarce
and instantaneously gone,
so you should maybe try
to appreciate them,
not squash their fiery
beauty into the ground
like cigarette butts."

Mysteries I'm Ready to Reveal

"You never held up your end of the bargain, you know."

"Pshhhht."

*"You said I could read your poetry.
You promised."*

"No, I didn't. I don't make promises."

"Well, can I?"

"Only if . . ."

"What?"

"I'm thinking.
. . .
Only if
you . . .
. . . stop
hurting
me so
much."

"How?"

"I'm not
your girlfriend
'n'
you're not
my boyfriend,
but
that doesn't mean
you should sleep with
other people."

"From now on, I only sleep with you."

"You Have to Understand

that a girl's words
are her soul, and
her soul is her heart.

A marble notebook is the hope
chest of the modern day.

You should know
that
opening these pages
is like
unbuttoning my skin,
and once
we go in,
we can never go back."

"I get it. I do."

Then he pulls that notebook
out of my grasp,
and fumbling
to get it open,
drops it
on the
dirty pink carpet of my room.

When He Reads My Words

He goes as silent as death
and touches
his forehead,
crinkles his brows
like
he's
thinking hard
thoughts.

Of course I've only shown him
the edited version.
I took out the
3 billion words
I've written about
him.

I read his expressions,
each immediate review:

When she lets me
see
what she's always scribbling
in that marble notebook,
well,
it's sort of a
disappointment—
not because it's bad,
because I don't know
the first thing,
but I know
I don't see a word
in here
about me.
And I'm looking.

The Slip

When I was little,
Mom dressed me up
in silk
and taffeta so
she could
show me off.

That's what church
is for, right?

Anyway, I remember
her tearing, smoothing, fixing
my childish stance before
standing back and taking me all in.

"Slip's showing,"

she'd say with
a grimace—disappointed that no
matter how she pushed
and pulled,
underneath I was
still
undisguisable,
messy
me.

When he
turns a page, "That Poem"
falls
from between the pages,
revealing EVERYTHING,

and I fidget;
I readjust
my plan,
but it's no use.

He's discovered
my flimsy paper secret
verse.

He beams
like a little league rookie
who just hit his first
home run.

Even the Air

is different
after he's undressed
my notebook.

Whenever we orbit each other,
his right hand swims
around my hand
like a fish wiggling
toward bait
until it envelops
mine.

Before,
he tentatively
teased my
peripheral vision.

Now he is
in my face,
against my skin,
on my mind.

One Afternoon

we collapse on a porch
swing, my head
in his lap,
his hands separating
my
   curls,
      one
    by
     one.

"What do you want to be when you grow up?"

"I don't want to grow up."

"What's the alternative?"

"Immortality, fame, plastic surgery . . .
What about you?"

"Same."

We Haven't Gone on a Date Yet

but I think we're in love.

I can't believe I just used
that word
un-ironically—
without a single
quotation mark.

I write about
him
all the time
lately.

Everything we do is a poem.

I've been consulting
the thesaurus for
synonyms
for him, like:

nubile, sultry, dishy,
and
bewitching.

Boys don't usually
make me look up
new words
to describe
them.

8 Things I Love

Her voice
Her voice saying my name
Her voice ripping Greg a new one
Her poetry
Her voice reading her poetry aloud
Her eyes
Her eyes reading my poetry
Her

On the House

I know how to mix a gin & tonic
perfectly,
just the way Mom likes it.
Tonight, she's being
difficult, hard to please, but
I'm a good
drink-tender.
I know how to
pretend
to listen
(learned it from her)
and increase
the alcohol
with each drink—
until the snoring starts.

Then, I can sneak out into my
cool secret,
my late-night
life.

He sits on the corner
where I'm hoping he'll be,
and I can't wait to sink down
next to him, smile, and forget,

but I can't forget.
I dwell and simmer
and eventually boil
over into tired tears.

He says, *"What, what, what—*
what is it?"

So I talk about
Mom
Dad
Sam
gin
tonic
and more,

but not about
Brian Kipley
because
some secrets
are just too
embarrassing.

He listens,
and then
says, *"What a*
bunch of
morons!"

He pulls me next to him,
stomps out his cigarette,
and says:
"Girl, you know,
you are
better than
a best friend. You
are more
than the sum of the parts
of your life.

Do you see that star?"

"That's Mars."

*"Exactly. Everybody else
are mere stars.
You, however, are the sky."*

"Like huge?"

*"No, like
you contain multitudes."*

First Clue

"What about your parents?" I'm laughing when I ask because of something he said before, but his face loses all its little bit of color.

"Assholes."

"It's like they were never young, you know?"

"If they were ever like us, that's the saddest think I've ever thought."

"What's that supposed to mean?"

"Trust me. I really, REALLY do not want to become my parents."

First Kiss

After
the crowd on the corner
dissolves,
and the nearest streetlight
goes black,
he asks
if he can
walk me home.

"You ready to give me a chance yet?"

"Ugh."

"What?"

"That's what you wrote in her social studies book."

"Yeah, but that was BS."

"And this is—"

"What's a guy got to do to get a girl like you?"

Then he slides
his thick, solid arm
around my waist
and turns me toward him.

First,
his lips graze mine
so slowly I tremble;
his stubble, so foreign,
tickles my cheek.

Then, his big hands
rest on my hips,
hold me steady

as if otherwise
I might float away.

His lips
beg
me
by brushing
over mine

again and again
'til I
give up
and open—

With his tongue,
he teaches me
how to shiver
from the
outside
in.

Good Morning

I wake up hard
with a mental picture of her. I don't know
if I dreamed it or remembered it
from the future. But this memory/dream
is a stain
that won't come out
of my mind: her wild hair splayed on a pillow
and all those
dark clothes finally peeled off her
pale
body.

I have to stay,
lie under the blanket for a while,
light a smoke, and just think.

Check the clock, it's only noon, so
I have to wait, but seeing her
is All I Can Think.

When I do, when I show up at her
house two minutes
after she's gotten off the bus,
I know my eyes must be
blazing, racing
like my heartbeat.
Another cigarette doesn't help.
My hands sweat as she
smiles and asks,
"What's wrong?"

"Nothing," I tell her,
"now."

Rendezvous

"Hello?"

"You're up.
Can I see you?"

"It's 3:30 in the morning . . ."

"I know."

". . . on a school night."

"So?
Isn't your mom passed out?"

Outside, I get the chills,
but not because of the frosty air.
Every footstep
sounds so loud
the night might
light up and unveil me.
Then I perceive his silhouette
in the triangle glow
of a streetlamp.
He walks toward me like a
tamer might
walk toward a spooked lion.

"Girl, my heart stops
when I see you;
I have whole
minutes
of sanity, I swear."

"Hey."

"One syllable
from you

is my
alcohol.

I get the
courage
to grab you
and kiss you
and make you
remember
me
like
I remember you."

View

We go
to the corner,
to the coffee shop,
to the woods,
to my bed
room, but
we never go
to his house—
not since that
day he opened
his notebook
to me.

I wonder
for a while,
and then I
ask why.

He changes the subject,
and he's got a million subjects.

But one day,
dark clouds
roll in and
block the sun.
Raindrops explode
like liquid bullets
down our backs.

We are so wet
we shiver,
but my house
is off-limits
(Mom's up), so

he leads me to
the back door
of his, and
in we sneak
directly
to his room.

I barely
see the dehydrated
flowers, the
framed heart prints,
the handmade
afghans
on the way.

Once we get
into his room,
he breathes.

He takes off his shirt first,
then my jacket,
unzipping, standing so close
I forget to inhale.

Even though
the heat is on,
I get chilly
bumps.

Only a few
molecules of
oxygen, a
polka-dot bra,
and a wet
T-shirt
separate
us.

He pulls off
his soaked-through
Levis and
leaves them
where they drop.

"Want a dry shirt?"

I nod, and he comes
over, grabs the soft hem
between bony fingers, and lifts
my wet Sex
Pistols shirt
over my head.

We stand body
to body
for a second before
he reaches behind me,
skin skimming me,
and abracadabras
a dry blue
cotton
tee
from his bed.

He pulls on
fresh jeans, grabs a shirt for himself,
but before he can
put it on,

thunder rolls through
the room: a deep, low
growl announces
the approach
of . . .

"My dad,"
he whispers.
His terrified expression
tells the rest of the story.

Truth is I'd never seen Random Boy
scared before that moment.

"They don't know
we're here," he
warns. He wraps
his strong arms
around my waist
and I feel
complete
-ly
safe.

I turn up my face
to kiss his chin,
and he pulls me
tighter.

We hide
behind his
bedroom door
while lightning
crashes in the next
room. I wonder what's
smashing, why he's
so ferocious. I flinch
and hold
my Boy. He
doesn't release
me until we hear
his mother

crying,
begging:

"Please stop. Please—"

He closes his eyes
and squeezes me
so hard it hurts.
I don't blame him
for hiding,
but
when he
lets me go,
flings open his bedroom door
and screams—
"Get off of her!"

—I realize I've got a hero
on my hands.

I watch from the
doorway as
he stands colossally
between
cowering
mother and
snarling father.

He clenches a fist
so close to his dad's
face, I wince.

"Leave. Her. Alone!"

The father/monster
looks amused. He
says, "Come here,
you pussy,"

grabs the Boy's neck, and
shoves his head down
so fast
I don't see
father/monster's knee
come up
to greet my Boy's
face. My fear
wants me to fly
as they fight, but
I make myself watch
instead. I make myself
be as still as stone. The one thing
I can't do now
is leave this Random Boy
alone.
I wish I were strong
enough to stop them.
I meet
Random Boy's eye
between two
fast-paced punches, a right, a left.
He winks at me—as if
it's all a show. He is not
being destroyed.

This Boy
is his mama's only defense,
and although it looks so, so bad,
he smiles a bloody-teeth smile
before he falls,
and his dad
finally
stops.

Mother/victim
—still on the ground—
rubs her side
for a minute
before insisting
it was nothing.
Everyone should forget this.

She eyes me suspiciously.

I cringe
in the doorway
and shake
when the monster sees me
standing out: a stranger at this
secret family meeting.

But Random
Boy reanimates, shaking it off
like a stubbed toe. His eyes flash up and
first thing they find is mine.
He rescues me with an outstretched hand
and a dizzy expression.
He re-invites me
back out
into the rain.

We go
where he likes to go
when he doesn't know
where to go.

I ask if he wants to talk
about it, but he only
buries his fractured head
in the crook of my neck and

cries like an animal
that knows
it's dying.

He only grips my hips
so I can't move.
And I don't care
because I don't want to move.
I don't want to run.

I know how it feels
to be your parents'
stupid mistake.

I want to un-break
him, too.

Shakes

I smoke less.
I can't finish a poem
without including your name
somehow.
I picture caged birds
and your empty pages.
I can't stop thinking of
your felt-tip miracles
just waiting to happen.

Shift

He's going to teach me how to drive.

He shows up in his dad's pickup,
a stick.
I say,
"Are you kidding me?"

(smirks)

He says I got to find the balance
between clutch and gas.
At the same time,
he slides his hand
over my thigh
and squeezes.

"Feel it?"

I stall out.

He laughs.

But when I keep stalling out,
he gets mad.

He reaches for the gearshift, relents,
then cradles his head
in his hands
like I'm hurting him.
He says nothing is wrong,
yet he shakes.

When I say it doesn't matter,
he gets madder. He
huffs and puffs
cigarettes

one after another.
I tell him:

"I don't want to learn from you.
You're a bad teacher."

I get out of the truck,
slam the door,
and walk home.

Couples Fight

and that's what we are,
though not
in so many words.

Truth is—
I don't get
how someone
so smart
can't do
something
so simple.

But after I sit in the passenger seat
for a while, thinking about
her hesitant turns,
her wide eyes,
I start to smile
and wish
she were still
here.

I start to feel like my lungs
are collapsing
without her
exhalations
to inhale.

So I return the truck
to the driveway,
silently,
exactly
as I found it.

I take a shortcut
to the corner

and inhale
the breeze
blowing by.

I find her

illuminated
red
in front of the Coke machine;
she is trying to decide.

"Sorry," I beg her.

She sighs,
chooses.

The can
loudly
  clunks
    down
      to
        her feet.

She bends, reaches,
and opens
it, takes a sip, and
hands the can over.

"What next?"

"You tell me."

Nightkissing

I never knew you
could memorize
someone's lips
with your tongue,
muscles
with palms,
or the intricate patterns
of fingerprints
with your
bare skin.

If school were like this,
I'd have better grades.

Justice

Everyone drops
away into the night
in couples and singles
and great big chunks of
curfew-bound
souls.

Somehow,
I convince her to stay.

"My mother," *she says,*
"will kill me."

"Would I
let that happen?"

(laughs)

"Good thing
I'm already dead."

Moonlight slides through the cracks
of our tree house ceiling
and
falls in sharp-edged shapes
and lines
on our
skin.

I only see these geometrical
pieces of her,
but
this is what I love:

Finally,
it is

just us

and the soft sounds
of wilderness.

Without all the civilized
threats of others,

I can lay my head
on her chest and hear
her
heart beat
only for me.

"Stay with me,"
I beg,
"all night."

(She takes a deep breath,
a fidgety
sigh
of
discontent.)

"What the hell,"
she whispers.
"She can't kill me twice."

We collide
softly
against
each other
all night,

but never break through.

"Young Lady"

I hate that term
of en-fear-ment.

She only calls me that
when I'm

unladylike.

"Where have you been all night?"

"I fell asleep at
a friend's house."

(Too transparently generic—
she sees right through
with her X-ray
Mom eyes.)

"I tried to call
but you didn't
answer," I say.

"You didn't call. What friend?"

"Mary."
I regret it
as soon as I say
it. If Mom checked,
who knows what Mary
might
say?

"Young lady,
congratulations!

You are now the
owner of a shiny new
curfew!"

You Know How

you wake up with a headache,
a pounding throb against
your skull that threatens
to manifest in your stomach
as an unstoppable puke,

but then
someone appears
with a cold, sweaty glass
of water and a few extra-
strength Tylenol and
tells you to lie back and let
the pain evaporate into oblivion.

You shut your eyes
feel the sharp
edges blur—

Love is when
someone allows you
escape
from it all
if only for a minute.

That's how my body reacts
to her running toward me,
wrapping her legs around me,
melting into my skin.

She's a pain killer,
addictive and sweet.

Sullen

"What's wrong?"
"*Nothing.*"
"Doesn't seem like nothing—"

(He scowls
at demons
I can't see.)

"Did I do something?"
"*No.*"
"Is it your parents?"
(silence)

"Yeah. Well, I don't want
to talk about your problems
anyway—"
(Secretly, I do. I do.)

I climb on his lap
and face him, let my legs
dangle on either side
of his.

I baby kiss his forehead,
bury more kisses in the curled-up ends
of his hair.

I stretch my arms around
his neck and squeeze so tight
that my body is
blocking out everything
but us.

He doesn't say anything.
His response is
purely physical.

Not the Problem

I don't know why
I give her
the silent treatment. I am
giving the world the
silent treatment,
and she catches
the ricochet.

The problem is the million obstacles
between us. The problem
is my parents.

My father
doesn't care
who's there,
he'll beat
my mother
for the stupidest
thing. For nothing
even.

If he touched Her,
I'd snap. I'd
blow. I'd go
black. And blue. And
blurry. I just know
I'd self-destruct
into so many pieces
I'd never get put back
together.

She won't be meeting the parents
again anytime soon. Or ever.

She can
take
away a lot
of shit. She can
probably save
me,
but even she
isn't strong enough to
stop
that
particular
hell.

Let Me

into your secret
world.
Show me the gates
you think
confine you.
I'll rip them down.

Show me your
deepest fear.
I'll kill it for you.

At the Laundromat

I slide my
Cougars hoodie
over my shoulders
and head,
add it to the pile
with the rest,
which means
I have to stand there
in nothing but a
snug white t-shirt,
threadbarely
covering
my black bra.

Looked fine in my room,
but now I wonder if it's
stupid
or pretty.

Even pooled together,
we have hardly enough change
to throw our jackets in a dryer.

We're only here because paying customers are
allowed
to soak up the free heat.

Everybody stares
at me
crossing my arms
over that blatantly black bra,
or maybe it just feels that way
because
Random Boy's eyes

are angry
almost.
My chills
get chillier.

Coming here was his idea,
but I can foresee
the fight we'll have later.

As we "enjoy" 12 minutes
of warm, dry, inside time,
Random Boy
seethes
silently;
it's
all
I
hear.

Finally,
when I pull that hot hoodie
over my frozen shoulders,
I feel safe.
Sometimes it's nice to have a roomy cotton
room where I can hide.

What She Doesn't Know

What she can't possibly know,
—'cause
who could do that
to someone
if she knew—
is that it feels
like knives slicing
my intestines
when I see a guy
lean toward her
so subtly
she doesn't notice
he's looking down her shirt.

She makes it too easy for them,
as though she wants it.
As though I'm not enough.

Under the fluorescent lights,
she blushes softly
at my stare,
and all I can
see is
how easily
she switched
from impossible dream
to mine,
and how easily
it seems
she'll turn right
back,
or away to one of these
guys
who cling, and stare, and touch.

Forewarning

*"It's not you.
It's me."*

"Are you kidding?"

"Actually, it's partly you."

"Oh, please."

"It's the way I react to you—"

"How's that?"

*"For the most part,
you make my fists loosen,*

*but sometimes,
I clench so tight,
I feel as though I'm going
to break.*

*So I apologize
in advance—
because
I will hurt you
a million times.*

*But I want you
to remember
I regret it
unconditionally.*

*Underneath all that—whatever it is—
is sorry, sorry
me."*

Nursery Rhyme

Mom, Mom,
go away.
Don't come back
some other day.
Get out of bed
and wash your face,
and run a sweeper
through this place.

Mom, Mom,
WTF?
Your little girl
is growing up.

Personal Graffiti

When the school bus steals you away,
I feel your magnetic soul
drag on mine,
and snap free.

It's a bad feeling.
A premonition?

I think we both know
you don't need no education.
You don't pay attention anyway.
You just carve us into your notebook.

Class Disturbed

Someone steals
my attention
from Ms. Jackson's
epic lecture
on epic poetry.

It's a boy,
staring blatantly
at his phone/camera/etc.
as he holds it up between our faces.

He pushes a button,
and I smize into his lens on instinct,
a move I've been practicing
in mirrors
since the fourth grade.

His eyes leave his screen
and meet mine over the phone;
he smiles.

"You,
have a beautiful profile,"
he says.

Never been told that before.

"Here, look . . ." He turns
his phone toward me
and swipes his thumb across the screen.
Beyond the pic from today
is a sideways view of me
reading,
then one of me writing,

and then another,
and another . . .

"Dude, you're a total
stalker."

"Sorry, I just think you're photogenic
and interesting.

I also have 296 pictures
of that sycamore—he waves to
the window behind him—
one for each day
I walked past it.
It's a . . .
     . . . different kind
of yearbook,
I guess."

We don't communicate
for the rest of class—

well, we don't talk—

but I watch him glide
through photographs of
street signs and cigarettes,
hands and toes,
trees and me.

I wonder how I never noticed him
noticing me.

I think when you're the kind of person
who feels she's been forgotten,
you don't see everything—
you forget yourself, too,
and you certainly don't

notice the ones who
remember you
so quietly.

As we're leaving class, he says,
"I like your shirt."
(I look down at Random Boy's
shrunken Buzzcocks T
tight against my boobs
and feel guilty.)

"I like yours, too."

(He's got a classic
rock thing
going on.)

"I also like how
you write in
short, straight
lines in print
so neat you
might be
a serial killer,"
he says.

Then he walks past me
and disappears
into the hallway masses.

Random Boy Meets My Mom

who eyes him like
chopped liver
on clearance.

He pulls me
close. She scowls.

"How long have you two been . . . ?"

"We're not boyfriend/girlfriend," I stutter.

"More like . . ."
(She stares at
only me.)
". . . soul mates."

She laughs bitter,
divorce-flavored
laughs.

She asks if his last name
belongs to the
couple she read about
in the paper.

His hunched shoulders
and bowed head,
his quiet yes
make me want to slap her.

"Well, it's nice
to meet you . . .
. . . I guess."

*"The feeling
is mutual,"*
he says

before grabbing my hand
and jerking me
out
side.

*"I can see
why you can't stand
to stay home."*

Why do his words
hurt
me?

All this time
I've wanted someone
to see,
but now
I wish he
were blind.

Hit Me Up

Next day
in school
while I am
daydreaming
instead of
note-taking,
something
hard and pointy
hits the back of
my head.

I turn
to find my
personal paparazzo
smiling at the
ceiling tiles.

When I unfold
the triangular
note,
I see his writing say:

"Truth is
I think you're
exceptionally beautiful
inside
and
out.
Can we hang
sometime?"

Peter X

What freaks me out most
about this boy
is how he provokes
indistinct fluttery feelings
in my head
when
he speaks,

as if his
voice
has mothy wings.

His words flap around
my brain long after he's gone.

I got a man,
yet
I get chills
when we brush hands
accidentally.

How can
that be
when I'm
already
in love
with my
Random Boy?

The guilt
is
unbearable,
but it's not
like

I can control
how I feel.

That
would
make
life
so
much
easier.

I want to write
about him,
but
given the
(Random Boy)
circumstances,
I shouldn't.

If only I didn't
have to write it all down,
but I do,
I do.

I don't
know why.

It just makes me feel better,
less alone with my thoughts:
less liable
to forget all the truth.

So I give him a code name.

Chills

Sometimes,
Random Boy
is very
un-random.

Sometimes, he is über-direct.

When he runs
his rough fingertips
across
   my
bare stomach,
it's like
raindrops
    falling
       fast
          and
             hard
on the dusty
diamond
of the
baseball field;
I go from stoic
to saturated
in seconds.

So
delicate—
only his nails
actually touch my skin,
or maybe the auras
of his fingers—
they skim higher
and higher

until
they reach
the round bottoms
of my breasts
by accident
seeming
almost.

At first,
a cool tingle
rushes
through my torso,
then
fire
gushes
everywhere.

Something Holds Her

back from holding me
as tightly as I cling
to her.

She won't call me
her boyfriend.

Something (or one) stands
between
us.

All I want
to do is
get her naked,
feel her
yield
completely.

All I want
is to be
indispensable
to her.

I ask around
at the corner.
I want to know
her secret stories—
the sleazy tales
she doesn't share.

They are few,
and all mostly unbelievable.
Brian Dumbass Kipley
says he banged

her before
we met.

My "friend"
Shane
says he'd like to—
but I shatter
his crooked admission
with an expression
he can't misconstrue.

At the coffee shop,
I mix
with the sugar and cream,
and interrogate
her classmates

who say

she's a loner,
drifting through cliques,
undefinable.

She hardly realizes
she's a
piece
of ass.

It's hard not to bash
in the cranium
of the asshole
who says those words,
but I remind myself
I'm under
cover.

I can't show
my fury. I don't want to
scare away
the facts
because I can't
hack the gossip,
so I listen
to truths and lies—
and try to decipher which is which.
The tension
builds in my brain,
down my arms
and hands,
until my fingers
begin to vibrate.

Alone

My Boy's got
a lot
of friends—
acquaintances,
people he knows
from parties
and deals,
from
living so much life
before I
busted out
onto his scene.

Even in school—
I notice eyes on me,
all the time appraising,
analyzing,
asking,
but not actually voicing
any questions aloud.

They don't accept
me, I think. I'm
just some girl who
appeared when
that guy
everybody
knows
noticed her.

They don't talk
to me.
Sure, I didn't
have any friends

before,
but now
it feels like
fewer.

Only eyes floating
up and down
the corridors,
slamming lockers,
walking,
looking away.

When I See His Name

in our notebook,
she might as well
be sleeping with him.

The deeper thrust
of the blade
is the shroud of protection
she's thrown over him
in the form of
a fake name—

Who the hell is Peter X?

He's every
one
and every
thing.

Every person
I see
enrages me.

Conjugation

We are supposed to be working
in groups, but let's face it:
group work is a Don't Ask
Don't Tell policy
between teachers and students.

Peter X
uses the time
to ask about my
family,
my "friends,"
my *je ne sais quoi,*
my favorite bands, the
writers I like,
movies I want to
see. And, oh,
what a coincidence,
he wants to see that one, too.

I doodle and Google and ogle
him all through my next class.

I open my notebook
and
write the story
of my mental
indiscretion,
empty my confusion
onto the page.

I read

I wait
and I
let her
crawl
deeper
into her lie.

I watch her
daydream,
and I wonder
who stars
in the mind-
movie she
watches
while she pretends
to watch movies
with me.

The fire intensifies
as I wait,
until . . .

Drawing Lines

At purple, hazy twilight,
he wakes groggy me
from a lingering nap.

He demands
to know
about Peter X.

I realize immediately
he's been
stalking
via marble notebook.

"Just a friend
from school."

He leans close
and whispers,

"I'll kill him,"

which makes me
simultaneously
cold
and
hot.

"He's my friend."

"But you didn't tell him about me, did you?"

(I don't know
what to say
or why

I didn't.)

"Honey"

(the name she calls me as the
ice clinks together
in her glass)

"I know
I'm not always
the best mother."

(Uh huh.)

"But this is me
trying—
no wait—"
She takes
a drink
to whet
the thinking
process.
I hope it works
'cause I could use someone
to talk to.

"I'm going to try harder.
I'm going to—

The thing is . . ."

(Sips)

Thanks, Mom.

I Love You So Much I'm Not Myself Anymore.

You know what I'll do
if you cheat?

I'll sharpen my knife
until the blade's
shaved so slender
it could slash
skin.

Then I'll find you—

You'll be
with him, of course
and I'll—

Peter X and I Have the Talk

"I have a boyfriend.
He's—"

"Wow. I didn't know.
You always look so—"

"Alone?"

"Well, yeah."

"I am,
even with the boyfriend."
(OMG, Shut! up!)

"Would he mind
if you talked
to me
about him?"

"Without a doubt."

"Then we won't tell him."

I stare at him,
confused,
and wonder if I can have my man
and enjoy this one, too.

What I mean is
I don't want to say good-bye
to the guy
who makes me forget the pain, but
I'd like to open
this door to a friend,
(who just happens to be a guy).

Got to find a way.

The Building

Since birth, really,
all I ever see
is sex
and sex
and sex.

It's on TV,
the subject of every joke.
It's on my friends' lips
and minds
all the time.

It's the reason
for every season,
the meaning of life.

It's in the air
as he & I kiss.
It's every
where
I go.

He sweats sex
and I dream
of orgasms
taking all our
troubles
away.

Sex is the
elephant
in the room
of our
togetherness.

It is the main idea
of my teenage paragraph:
make love, hook up, do it, bang, etc., etc., etc.

To be honest,
I'm sick of it
and I haven't even done it
yet.

I tend to get obsessed
with songs and movies and
people. Right now,
I'm possessed
by sex
and not knowing

what it will do
to me & you.

Questions I Don't Ask

Seems like I should
consult a manual
or tell someone
before

I go through with it.

I fixate:
Should I?
Will it hurt?
Is he
the right
one?

I make a decision,
and an appointment
at the place
where they give out
free condoms
and advice.

What I notice most
about that place
is how no one makes
eye contact—

I don't feel judged
like I thought I would.
I don't even feel
seen.

Inside the tiny cubicle,
as I'm answering
form questions,
I can hear the

girl-next-door
telling her secret
love stories:

"How many partners?"
"Eleven."

I have a list of doubts
etched on my mind:

What is it like . . . exactly?
How does it feel before . . . during . . . and . . .
Will he change?
Will I?
Is this right?
How do you know?
Should I?
When should I?
How should I?
What if I cry?

But there's
no time
for stupid questions,
no box on the form
to check for uncertainty,
no truth about love
in stirrups.

Seriously, it's like backstage:
where you can see all the magic
is made up
of holograms
and mirrors.

It's
wham,
bam,
here you go, ma'am.

I open the pill pack—
tiny pink circles of responsibility—
and unfold the directions,

and as I studiously read
the million crinkly words
about percentages,
I find
not one honest answer
to a real question.

Honestly

I don't know if I should,
but I will,
'cause maybe, just maybe,
this
can make it all right.

It's worth a try.

"All I Want to Know Is

do you love me?"

"Do you have to ask?"

"It would seem."

"Yes."

"That's it?"

*"Girl, I would lay my leather jacket across acid-rain
puddles for you,
rescue you from atomic-bombed buildings,
and ride into your high school
on a white motorcycle
if I could."*

"Yeah, but that's all make-believe.
I mean really, truly, absolutely—
am I special?
Or am I the
same
as
everybody
else?"

*"Girl, when I first
saw you,
I tried to wake the
hell up.
I rubbed my eyes.*

I thought you were a dream."

"But I'm not."

"You're better."

"But how do you know?"

"Know what?"

"That you won't . . .
whatever this is"
(I move my hand in a little circle
close to his heart)
"won't die
like everything else."

Promise

Girl, I'm not your daddy.
I'm not going to leave
no matter how hard
you push me away.

But See

Why's he got to go
bringing my dad into this?

It's like he means to say
I love you—
but it comes out
a sharp-edged
sword
instead.

I know
he means well,
I think.

Up 'til Now

she's always turned bone
dry when it came up.

Word on the street
is
she's not
a virgin,
but
her raw
shivers underneath
my hands tell
a different story.

I want to
take her,
and if she leads
the way, I will.

But I'm terrified
I'll screw
her up.

So every time
we get too close,
I turn
off
and
away.

Let's Talk About Fear

"What scares you?"

"Everything."

"For real."

"Regret. That I'm doing something now I'll reg
later."

"You mean me."

"I'm not doing you."
(nervous laughs)
"No, I mean—"
(but he's partly right)

"What scares you?"

"That for you this is a game."

"What?"

*"Me.
I know you're going
to straighten up
and leave
me one day,
so I can't relax.*

*My biggest fear
is you, or rather
the absence of you."*

Mapping the Course

Like a hundred thousand pins
barely pushing in
every city on my skin:

He says no when I tell him
yes.
He says
he's not ready,
"but," he says, relenting, *"since you're ready—"*
and he shivers.

He strips me slowly
and travels me with eyes wide
open. He explores
and marks me—
biting and pressing
like a hundred thousand pins.

That's how it feels
when his fingers
and his tongue
run marathons
up and down
my back, my belly,
then farther
down
to
curves
I didn't know
I had
before he
kissed
them.

In a Tree House

The plywood boards
nailed together by previous
generations
show their years
of rain and pain
and kids
who should've known better.

Yet, I climb
the ladder
behind him.

He's brought blankets
that smell like him,
TastyKakes,
and a six-pack of ice-cold
generic soda.

He even lit a candle
so I can see
the clean-wood rectangles
on the walls
where the centerfolds
once hung.

We kiss,
hug, play
a game of hide-
and-seek,
so to speak,
and then

I take control:
I blow out
the candle
and roll my back

onto the sleeping bag
he's brought.

"It's time," I tell him, pulling him
(so strong yet so easily moved)
on top of me.

"Are you sure?"
"I want to."

Then so slowly,
so carefully,
he—

. . .

It isn't the heavy breathing
scream-fest
they make it out to be,

and the pain
wasn't half as bad as
watching my father leave.

For me,
anyway,
it was warm and very quietly
intense,
like being between the pages of
a book
I've been dying to read—
one that makes me close
my eyes sometimes, to stop
and just to wonder
whether it
lives up
to the hype.

It Was Like

for the longest time
I didn't want to sleep
with her
because sex
is something
too ordinary
for us.

But the main thing
holding me back
is how,
afterward,
girls change.

It's more than great,
but sometimes,
it's not
even worth the hassle.

But tell me that
in the midst
of some chick
saying yes.

Only when she said yes
was I so scared
I had
to resist.

Anyway,
that's not the point.

The point is that
when I was naked and kissing her
under the stars last night,

she took me in
her hands, and
pulled me
in—
impossible
to
argue—
and it was

different.

Most amazing:
She didn't change.
She didn't do
any of the things
I expected
like cry, or pout,
or regret it.

Afterward,

she lit two of my
cigarettes with
a single flame, and
passed me one.

Her naked skin glowed
in the orange light,
a million times more
beautiful than
the picture I'd dreamed.

I mean,
there are times
when it's over
and the

colorful girl
you came in with
turns black and white
like The Wizard of Oz *in reverse,*
but that didn't happen with her.

Don't get me wrong;
I've had a lot of sex,
but now I know
what it's like
to lose
my virginity.

In Vino Veritas

Mary passes me the
truth serum
she stole from
her parents'
secret stash.

"If you weren't sure
you were ready,
why'd you do it?"

I don't answer her.
I don't even know why I told her.
I had to tell somebody.
I answer her question in my own head:

He had this
expression
I recognized.
Would be easiest
to call it hunger,
but it also had touches
of lunacy
and confusion
and one heartbreaking
question
only I could answer.

I felt so powerful.

For the first time,
sex
didn't
seem like
the first prize

in a beauty pageant
or
—a teenage cliché—

it didn't feel like the ball
in a game of keep-away.

It felt like a pretty, wrapped-up
gift only I could give
to take
all the insecurity
away.

And it did
for him
for a while.

Valentine, Incognito

When I go to the printer
to wait for my
chem-lab notes,
I have to pass Peter X.

I know it's probably ridiculous,
but I wonder
if I walk differently
now that I've . . .

I keep wondering
if people can tell,
if I can notice
a difference.

He smiles as if
he has a secret,
too.

At the printer,
where the paper
emerges, I find
on top of the pile

a freshly printed
  photo mosaic
      heart

made up
of tiny close-up
pictures of my
hair/cheeks/lips/hands/etc.,
every part of me, but my eyes.

On my way back,
I thank him
bashfully.

I beam.
I'm so happy he
still
cares
for some reason.

He moves his phone
in circles
and
says,
"I didn't include
any pictures of
your eyes
'cause they're
too hard to catch."

Mirror

I don't look
like your typical
dude-magnet.
I've got uncontrollable
hair and pale skin
that some people

(okay—one person)

call luminescent. I've
got a problem
making choices
that might last
forever,
a.k.a.
all of them.

My feelings sometimes

(okay—MOST times)

are like friends who won't shut up
and let good enough be.

What am I trying to say?

Just that . . .

. . . sometimes, I find myself
daydreaming . . .
of other lives
I'm destined for,
lives so much different than
mine.

Sometimes I catch my brain
knowing, just knowing
(waiting for the rest of me to admit)
that even though I love him,

15

might be
too young
to say
forever

but I keep saying it.

Abruptly

I am aware
of how little
he knows
about my
in-school
life—how
Ms. Jackson
thinks I could be
a writer one day,
how Peter X
helped me pass
my chem test,
how I am failing
phys ed
because
I keep forgetting
to retrieve the gym uniform
Random Boy peeled off me
weeks ago and
never returned. He
sent me home in a
Ween shirt instead.

School has become my secret, safe room
away from it all,
where I am different,
where I can open up my body/soul windows
and let the difference out.

Skipping

Girl, why
don't you
not leave me
tomorrow?

Why don't you
stay home and make
love to me all day?

I hate when you
go,
and I know
you
hate it, too.

So why don't you
skip? I'll
take you places
you dream
about. I'll make
you want to
drop out
altogether.

Boy, hello?
Welcome to the
21st century.
You can't get a
library card
without a
diploma.

You got time
to write a thousand poems.
How 'bout you make
time for me?

Undecided

It's like I'm his favorite
color and he never wants
to let me out of his sight. Only

I'm not sure he's the best shade for me.

I kind of want to try chartreuse (which he says
there)
or aqua (which he says is *gay*).

Maybe *I'm* gay;
guess
I'll never know.

Worlds Collide

He takes me on a date
date—the kind where
he borrows his dad's
truck, cleans it, and
opens its doors for me
when he picks me up.

At the restaurant, he
asks me for advice on
what to order.
I can't help but smile
at the buttons
buttoned on his shirt.

We pick at each other's
dishes and fill up before
everything we ordered's
been served.
We balance too many
Styrofoam boxes as we exit.
Someone holds the door
open for us. "Surprise!"

It's, uh . . .

"Hey, how you
doing? Fancy meeting you
here!" (big innocent smile)

"Hey." I rush rush rush to the
car, hoping he won't ask.

"Who was that?"

"Uh, no one,"
I say, just as Peter X runs
up behind me and places a
tiny white box on top of the
others.

"You dropped this," he says,
making deep eye contact.

"Oh, are you sure?"

"Yeah," he says, "I took a picture
of it falling.
Want to see?"
He turns.
"This must be—"

"Who was that?"

"Just a boy from school—"

I say his Real Name
out loud and Random
Boy makes fun of it.

I wish I could erase
Peter X from my
notebook, but
not from my life.

"What did he mean?
Why did he say
he took a picture?"

"He always takes pictures
of everyone,"
I lie. "He's a total freak."

I feel bad
piling up untruths,
but this dishonesty pyramid
is the sturdiest protection
I can build
for Peter X.

The Peter X Thing

hangs
in the truck
like a noose.

I wait

for him
to speak,
to sentence
me to payback
for knowing a person
he knows nothing
about

so I can get it over with.

Instead, he gives me
radio silence

for a good ten minutes,
the turn signal so loud
and long
and insistent,
it makes me nauseous.

*"That dude
is a douchebag,"*
he says matter-of-factly.
"You know him from school?"

"From chem."

"I hope he's not your school boyfriend."

"My what?"

"The X-man you write about."

146

I throw my hair back
against the headrest
and sigh.

We were having a
good night.

"Just tell me."

"What?"

"You love me."

"More than myself,"
I say.

It seems
truer
every day.

The Drive Home

is quiet and uncomfortable

until we both try
to turn on the radio
and our fingers
greet each other
at the scan button.

A song we love
happens to begin
and we settle in—
my off-key voice reaching over
the armrest to remind him
I'm here.

His secretly beautiful
voice
doesn't
sing back.

He pulls over,
puts us in park,
but leaves the engine going,
the music flowing through
the cab
as he rolls down the windows,
sending the food smells out
and the cool air in.

He leans over and
kisses me deeply—
breathes me.

His hand cups the nape
of my neck
as the other
     slides
between T-shirt
          and skin.

Right there,
next to frenetic weeknight traffic,
an electronic DJ
spins a song
with a bass line
straight
from hell
and we dance
sort of.

We use it as the backbone
of our movements, our
quick, desperate
grasps
for that thing
we both know
exists
when we're together
but that we can't seem
to locate lately.

Random Boy yanks
the shirt over my head,
exposing me
to the headlights going nowhere,
striking my skin

—radiant whips—
   as they pass.

We
get naked fast, and
as the singer
croons the bridge,

he and I
dissolve our differences
and
become
one—
a resounding song echoing
on a dark night.

Next Day

I spend
study period
in the library.

Maybe I'm avoiding Peter X.

I breathe fresh
old-book air
until
a cloud rolls
between the windows
and me.

"Hi, Brian,"
I say, hoping
he'll keep rolling by,

but he sits
and eyes
my marble notebook
and me
with a sick smile.

"Hi, yourself.
So guess whose tits
I saw on the side of the
highway
last night?"

He laughs,
and I envision
wild animals shriveling
prey
with dirty teeth.

"Never knew
you
were such a
slut is all.

Well, when that
Prince Charming of yours—"
(snorts)
"dumps you,
hit me up,
kay?"

I don't know what to say—
so get this:

I say
nothing.
I get up
and walk
away.

And that night,
when Random Boy
asks about my day,
I keep quiet.

I don't know why.

Mindf*cking

We have sex so much it hurts,
but whatever. When we go
a whole day without, he worries
I don't love him anymore.

It's as if the closer we get, the
more he needs to be reassured.
I sigh 'cause I don't know
what else to do, which

just makes him madder.

Then, one late, smoky night,
while our laughter still lingers
from a private joke,
he asks, *"Would you rather
be with someone else?"*

Like I'd say so if I did.

"Yeah right," I say.
"Like who?"
"Like Brian Kipley."
"Like what? Why him?"

I am shivering I'm so cold.

*"'Cause he told me
he screwed you some night
in a tent
at a keg party
in the woods."*

"My dad had just left."

"So it's true?"

I don't tell him it's not,
even though it's not—
true.

Let him deal with knowing
what it's like
to love a slut
for a while.

Boom Shaka Lak

She's being a bitch
and I don't know why.
I try
to kiss it out of her,
to tempt the truth
from between her legs.

Anger turns to
desperation,
which seems like
it could turn to
death
at any time.

Mine. Hers. Ours.

I black out sometimes,
but that's not the surprising part.
I'm shocked
when I come back
to find
I'm still alive,
and she's still here, too.

Ever After

Since we did it,
all he wants to do
is do it
again
and again, when all
I want is him
to beg me
again, not
expect me to
open up, sesame
every time; it's
like all the what if
is gone. He's
reached the end
of the story, but I
keep flipping pages,
thinking
he might
write me
something new,
some words less
blue
than I'm used to.

But no, he picks me
up and drives me
to the nearest
bed, where he
beds me before
he says a
word.

Peek

Usually,
I slam the door
shut
to the outside.

You see,
I don't allow
spectators
at the peep show
of my life's lousy
moments, but
I want to show

you

the worst parts.
I want you to know
where I go
when I won't
let you
follow.

I know I said it's about
eating, sleeping, and sex—
but not with you.

Sex used to be my
biological requirement,
but now
it's a spiritual quest—
at the end is
the most powerful
peace.

So here's what I'd tell you
if I had any guts:

Usually,
my dad relents
before I get
involved.

He knows
I have a boiling point
he can push me
to. It's not written
in stone. It's
an understanding
between men.

Usually,
he respects
my anger

because
usually,
I stick up for
my mother.

Not usually—
every goddamn time.

And sometimes I think it's
some kind of training
for life.

Today, though
when my old man
turned on me,
when he
surprised me

from behind
with an old metal pipe
destined for
the junkyard,
she
didn't
open her mouth, she
didn't even pretend
to pull him off.

She just
watched
from the
floor beside
the coffee table
while he
beat
the living shit
out of me
with a metal
goddamn
pipe.

I guess I'm not surprised.
She's beat down
inside and out.
Defending me
would just be an invitation for
him to target her
instead.

I didn't fight
back. I
let the strikes
blast

against
my skin, detonate
the suspicions
I've held
all my life.

From the outside,
it must have seemed
like I didn't even
hurt.

But all the while

—this is what I want
you to remember—

I fought
to keep
alive—
that's what I was doing.

I was holding your innocent image in
a glass ball in the center of my skull.

That was all I thought about.

You see,
I want you
to remember what I REALLY am

even as I feel myself changing.

Then

one Wednesday night,
between fights,
we find ourselves
at the playground,

acting
like
children.

He pushes me
on the swing
while we take turns
swigging
from
a flask.

We laugh
genuinely
at each other's
smiling.

We have actual fun.

He says,
"Be honest with me—"
with an unfamiliar tilt of his head,

and imagine this: everything
about him
is altered. He is
almost a stranger, but more like
a friend
I haven't talked to in an eon.

So I am honest,
not vindictive—

when I tell him
my embarrassing secrets
about Brian, the truth
about that long-ago night,
about his horrible words in
the library
last week.

I am so honest, I weep.
I wait for him to get mad
about letting a jerk like Brian
touch me.

He listens,
and walks
around the swing;
I am reeling through the cold
air toward him now.

"Girl,"
(He gets on his knees)
"I'm so sorry
you got to
deal
with that bullshit.

I'm so sorry
you got to put up with
me."

The swinging
weakens. No matter how
you push, the laws of physics
always win.
My feet
skid against the dry dirt

until I am a soft, still spot
in this hard, edgy night. His
head begs its way into my lap,
his hands swim around
my waist. I reach down and touch
my ice-cold fingertips
to his warm neck.

Is he crying? He is.
His heart reposes
in my hands.

*"Why does
it have to be—"*

He doesn't finish.
He doesn't have to.

Silently, we move
like wind chimes in autumn,
creating some sort of music
as we barely
and entirely
touch.

Descent

Typical night on the corner:
I must have smoked 17 cigarettes
by the time he randomly showed up.

It's like he's sewn a voodoo doll
of my heart. And he likes to poke
it, watch me squirm and effervesce.

You know how two pairs of eyes
can be on each other, even though
their people are far apart?

That's how it was with us.
He didn't say a word to me, but
man, he was screaming with his eyes.

The big surprise did not appear
until the next morning, on the school
bus ride. Brian Kipley

climbed on the bus with the most
busted-up face anyone anywhere has ever
seen. And I just sunk down
                    down
                        down in my seat.

Ugh

I didn't do that to his face,
so why do I feel responsible?

It's like that's the consequence of
telling the truth
about a boy
to a boy.

I didn't mean to sentence Brian
to Random Boy's wrath.

From now on,
I'll lie.

It's the only way
to be safe.

Note

You tell me one thing,
then I read your notebook
and it turns out you're
a liar.

Now, how can I
trust
someone
who lies
so easily?

I love you.
I want to help you,
but sometimes I worry
you're too far gone.

P.S., I only say so because I love you so much.

Communication

I don't think
it's cute
when you read my
notebook
without
me knowing.

But you
showed
it to me
once.

Yeah,
once.

Okay.

. . .

First of all, you can look at my notebook whenever you
want—any page—I got nothing to hide.

But as for yours,

I'll
never
read
it
again.

Even if you want me to.

P.S.

When you read my notebook
it's like I can't be alone—
not even
in my own head.

It's like you
already have
my body
and now
you want
my mind, too.

Get your own mind, K?

Turns Out

That guy at the restaurant is her secret X-man,
the dude she never talks about,
but writes about
ALL THE TIME.

I know because
I've got friends
who look out
for me. They don't
want to see me hurt.

The vibrating hands
reach a crescendo.

I can no longer—

Truth

I hate him.
I don't remember loving him
Truth is: I think I'm deluded.
I think I must want pain and
crave punishment.

After what he did,
I don't ever want to see his stupid face again.

Good to know.

I thought you weren't going to read my notebo
anymore.

You caught me.
I couldn't resist the title.

What He Did

I don't want to talk about it.

Let's just say
I can't
believe it.

I never
thought
—never ever—
he could
hurt
me
that badly.

Honestly

You think I want to feel
this way about you?
Man, I used to eat
chicks for breakfast
and now they spring up
everywhere wanting me
to screw
you over,
but
I'm too busy wrapping
myself around your
pinky to respond.

I don't know how
you can be jealous.

Don't you see that
I can't love anything
on this planet
more than

You?

Clarification

It's not
jealousy. I'm
used to you
and most of your ways.

It's more about the
fact that
you held me down
and wouldn't let me go
for an hour, made me
listen to a screaming,
hateful
list of all the
things that are
wrong
with me.

You left marks on my arms,
you were so rough

(and indelible stains on us).

It's not about
jealousy

anymore.

Temper

I'm stronger than I want to be.
My rage lately
is a conflagration
out of control.
My emotions, bottled tight,
are exploding
like shook-up champagne.

I keep waiting for someone
to notice the noise
my head makes.

I can go on
making comparisons
but they all mean the same thing:

I am not me.

She is the animate object of my affection.

And I do regret
the monster I've become,
whom neither of us love.

I regret him,
but truly,
if I'm being
honest,
I rely
on him.

Only he can make her see
how much she tortures me.

Physical Description

I don't give details
because it's
a gray, hazy
thing,
but

it feels and
sounds
like being crunched
in his giant,
contracting
fist.

It happens so fast
I can't tell
exactly
which hand
is striking me,
and I don't know
which muscles
to clench,
which way to turn
to get away,
so I just shrink
and sink into
a "happy" place,
and
hope
it ends
quickly.

You want details?

One time
when he didn't like
what I said,
he grabbed my throat
with one hand.

Did you know
a breathing tube
is as easy to crush
as an aluminum can?

He squeezed until
I couldn't talk,
couldn't beg him
to stop. He held on
for so long, I got a
taste of what it's like
to die
unsatisfied.
Everything
went black.

. . .

I woke up to him
kicking me,
saying:
"Get up.
Stop
faking,
you lying
bitch."

Recovery

The weird thing is . . .

I don't feel any pain
'til later, when we're
lying in the grass
after make-up sex.

He didn't notice
how I didn't
really want to do it,
that I was just
so grateful
his hands were
tender
for a change.

I cried. Him, too.

He begged me things I didn't understand:

"Help me," he kept saying.
"Where am I?" he asked once.

Could I leave
someone
asking me that?

His lips moved
slowly
over each bruise,
trying to take
away completely
—the hurt—

but he couldn't.

In so many ways,
my body is just a surface
he can't break through.

Fatally Wounded by a Stray Bullet

Maybe it's like she says,
I don't know.
For me, it's like
blood seeping into
my vision.
Everything
disappears
and all I can
do is grope my way
through
the red.

I am so, so
sorry if I hurt her. Really,
honestly,
I mean to hurt
myself. She just
gets caught
in the
cross-self-fire.

Tongue Tied

I told him
next time
he did it,
I'd leave.

I meant it,
but I don't think
he believed me.

I don't know
if I believe me.

I don't know
why I said that
anyway.

What
I meant to say
was,

Get out of my life.
I hate you.

So why didn't I?

Pictures

We go to the drive-ins,
and lie in the bed of
the truck, softened
by piles of blankets
that smell like us.

Looking up at the
giant illuminated love
story, I start to get
dizzy—maybe because
I recognize the signs.

I can see it coming
before the characters,
a married couple,
wrestle
to the ground.

He slaps
her hard, the clap
echoing off
the cars around us.

Random Boy
squeezes my hand
so hard, I hurt.

If I Had Someone to Tell

Would I?

Like Mary,
who secretly
crushes on the
randomness of
Random Boy
and is crushed
by the un-
believable
fact that
he chose
me?

Like his
best
friend,
who
won't
look me in the eye?

Like the kids
at school
who
ignore
me more
each day?

Like
Mom,
who is
as delicate
as cigarette
ash these days,
but much less easy
to talk to?

"I Know What's Going On"

At the sound,
my hand moves straight
to the bruise on my thigh.

"Obviously
that boy is
having sex with you."

Oh.

(How can she tell? Is the
evidence
in the ways I
walk/talk/stalk
about him?)

"Yeah."

"Thanks for talking
to me about it. Remember
when you promised to involve
me in all your Big Life Decisions?"

"No."

"You were 5."

?

"Now, there's only one
thing I can do."

Offer advice?
Ask me how I am
coping
with the decision?

"I made you
an appointment
at Planned Parenthood.

They'll take care of you."

I don't tell her I've been on the
pill for a few months
already.

I'm in
love,
but I'm not stupid

usually.

Confession

I tell Peter X
how mean
Random Boy
can be, but
I don't tell
him

the whole truth

because some
secrets
are just
too embarrassing.

He doesn't get
why I sell myself
short
(his words),
why I don't just
end it
if it's imperfect.

"We have all our lives
to settle,"
he says.
"For now,
you should be
finicky."

He leans in close
to an anthill
and takes a pic
of a tiny bug
carrying three times
its weight.

It probably won't
come out.

"You should be
with somebody
who sees
you

like I
do."

Snap.

Justify

When it's good,
it's real good,
like two different
delicious flavors
of ice cream
becoming one
awesome
new taste
you never
heard of.

But when it's bad,
it looks like broken teeth,
tastes like blood,
smells like death.

It sucks like war.

Everything
we love
gets ruined.

But when it's good—
well I'm pretty sure
(if you want to know why
I'm still here),
love doesn't
get any realer
than the
violent,
jealous kind.

And right now,
I want just two things:
real and love.

See, everything
is a give, take.

Sometimes when you're touching
the fiery center of real love,
you get burned.

Limits

Don't wear that.
Don't drink that.
Don't talk to him.
Don't listen to that.
Don't smoke that.
Don't be like that.
Don't eat that stuff.
Don't say those things.
Don't write about me.
Why don't you
write about me?
Don't tell me
you just want your
freedom
back.
Don't.
Just don't.
Why are you doing that?
Because I want to
It's so gay. Why would you want to?
And so on
and so on
and on and . . .
. . . so on,
etc.

Possessed

"Girl,
why won't you
give?
I don't lie
when I say I'd die
for you.

Stay true, and I'll lie
down and
forget everything
but you."

"Give what?
What don't I give?

I don't want
an empty shell
of you.
I want
the stranger
who surprises,
the Random Boy
in the crowd
at
the corner."

"That dude?
He wasn't nothing
'til you came
along—"

"Don't be
double negative."

"And that corner?
It's dead—
a toxic wasteland.

Say so.
Say you'll grow old with me."

"I don't want to grow old with you.
Stay young with me."

"You are
too good
for—"

"Boy, can't we
be
us,
and still be
you & me
separately?"

"You are mine—
nothing (not/even/space)
comes between
us."

What I Don't Get

is how he can
love me
and also hate me
so much
he
hurts
me.

He hugs me
so tight,
he squeezes
all the me
out.

What They Don't Mention in the Caution Tales

is how lonely life gets,
and how sometimes
even though people suck,
if it means
you don't have to be
alone,
you'll take 'em.

As much as he loves
is as hard as he hits,
which makes the pain
reassuring
in a sick way.

You know,
some days
I see me
as a
victim
in an unjust
attack;
other days
I wonder if
I am the
antagonist
he says I am
or—

Maybe, just maybe,
I am
the protagonist
of my own life story.

Regardless,
somebody forgot
to cast me
a supportive best friend.

Quiz

He doesn't love me.
He doesn't need me.
He cheats on me.
~~I'm not~~ *He's not* good enough for ~~him~~ *me.*
We should break up.

False.
False.
False.
True.
False.

Sign Language

He hesitates.

His fingers move
forward and back
on my skin.

I encourage him

to come in
by turning over
my forearm
like a new leaf.

His fingers graze
the delicate skin,
tickling me through
my entire body/soul.

We could not speak
for days
and still know
all there is
to know
about
each other.

Reconnaissance

Lately,
life is a murky
swamp
obscured. What I mean is,

Mom cries
all the time.

She's stopped
cooking and cleaning
and looking clean as well.
She's stopped
functioning
really.

Dad drinks ALL his meals
now.

Mom is so beaten down,
Dad doesn't even beat her
anymore.

Now me—
that's another story.

It's like
World War Whatever
up in here.

Sometimes I don't
come home, I roam
all night, check
for lights
in my Girl's window.
She writes all night.

That marble notebook
is like another man.

I watch them, but

somehow,
she can't feel me
down here
in the depths,
needing

her.

Healing

Yesterday,
he blew up
worse than ever.
My right
side still hurts.
My hands wouldn't,
couldn't
write a word
about it
until today.

Maybe I shouldn't write
about it at all.

I know I said
I'd leave,
but
I love him
and
I know
he can be
good
some day.

Most of all, I'm afraid, though,
that
no one
could ever
love me that much
again.

Cupid

He hits,
but always misses
the mark.

When he puts his big
hands on me, I feel
small:
skinny,
pale,
easily broken,
but
the thing is—
that thing that surprises
even me?

I don't break;
I bend.

Here's the thing:

He hugs
so hard, but still
can't squeeze free the
solid seed
of my heart.

Crush
all you can, love,
it
won't
die.
I won't let it.

So why do I close my eyes
to the obvious?

Because
when he hits,
the love
he lets me have
after
is amplified.

It's like I feel MORE when
my skin is bruised,
when my blood
bubbles up to
the surface;
it warms me so I
can melt him
to tears.

When we're right there,
in the bluest portion
of the flame,
it's the best
kind of love.

I can barely feel
the hate.

Thinking

The worst part
is when
you scold me
with various versions of:
You're a bitch
who only cares about herself.

I think it might be true.
Sometimes, I feel like I have to pick:
me or you.

Our love is changing
into something else,
something permanent,
and the change feels like
a swirling tornado
in my gut—

Who would let someone
do this to her,
and then crawl back
into his still-shaking arms?

People
in love
wouldn't do this
to each other,

and I'm too young
to turn into my mother.

Eye Witness

Peter X
could tell something
was up. He saw me writing
frantically in my marble notebook
and asked if my muse was in town.

You know how boys flirt in the most unconven
ways?

Peter X grabs
the book
from my desk
and flip dee doos
through my life/pages
like they're nothing
but paper.

"Don't," I say,
struggling
to reach—

Pushing me
playfully away,
he grasps my shoulder
—nothing really—
unless you're as bruised
as a month-old peach.

Seeing me wince, he pulls
back pitifully
and asks,

"Everything okay?"

But my shirt has
slipped over my shoulder

and there on my pale-
skin canvas are painted
purple fingerprint stories,
evidence
of the most
recent
crime committed.

I can make up
excuses like
you wouldn't believe, but
I don't.

It's easier to lie to myself
than to Peter X.

And for a brief second
it's like I'm a cartoon,
and he's not Peter X at all.
He's relief
personified.
He's a door
left open
on a deserted
road.

Truth-telling

Because I didn't
prove my love
to his satisfaction,
he grabbed my wrists
and squeezed them
together in one of his fists.

He told me not to move,
like I had a choice.

Because I didn't
tell him I wasn't
going to show,
he found me
and made me
sorry.

Because I
am a "stupid
little slut"
(his words),
I have these
scarlet
letters
on my
shoulder.

Because,
because,
because.

"What Happened?"

In the library,
between the stacks,
we stare into each other's
dubious eyes.

"Why would you put up with that?"

Ugh.

"I don't get it."

Me neither.

"You don't have to—"

"Don't I?"

"Do you think he's the best you can do?"

"What's that supposed to mean?"

"I wasn't going to tell you because you're
. . . involved . . .
but I like you—"

"But he loves me, and I love him, too."

(As I repeat this mantra,
the picture in my head
is movie-esque.
We are outcasts—together.

I could never imagine
myself
in some everyday
casual romance
with Peter X,
who knows just what to say.)

"But I wouldn't hurt you—"

Before I can stop him,
he takes out that camera
and snaps.

"What are you doing?"

"It's just—I wish I could make people see
how the world looks to me.

It's why I take so many pictures.

When I stop,
take a picture, and stare,
I see how so many
giant fiascos
began with some
tiny, out-of-sync
detail
no one noticed.
They're always there:
a million pixel-sized clues."

He scrolls through a brief visual history of me
on his phone.
We both watch
me go from
unaware dreamer
to smizer
to some sad chick.
I don't recognize her.

I don't know what he intends
with this slideshow,
but suddenly what scares me most
is how much he knows.

Something Happens

I avoid Peter X at school,
ignore his unabashed,
accusatory glower.

With Random Boy, it's like
someone knowing
has brought us closer.
I tumble in his
open palm,
crash
like a waterfall
down his rib cage,
and drip through
his fingers.
I eatsleepbreathe him
and never turn him away.

I can't explain it
only to say
that he is my
imperfect darling,
and I, his. If we
don't overprotect
one another,
who will?

Mom Wants to Know

why I'm moping around
in sweats while

she kneels
in front of the
open fridge,
scraping coagulated jelly
from glass shelves. The interior
light illuminates her face.

"You look good, Mom."

"Thanks. Wish I could say
the same for you."

She eyes me, and
I despise me
a little more.

"Thanks?"

"Why don't you
call up your girl
friends and go
to the mall or
the movies or . . .
Do you want to
try that new Thai
place with me?"

I've been dying
to try
something different.

A question mark
hangs in the air,

a curly request
for more information.

Maybe we could talk
about things
over dinner;
maybe we could talk
period.

But how would I word it?
What would she think
of me?

I walk away from her
interrogation and
slide into bed.
I spill my secrets
to the blankets,
to my pages
and sheets.

Mom comes to the door
and doesn't say anything.

Finally, she knocks
just once. "I'm here
now
if you need me."

Even Mary

notices the absence
of my smile these days.

"Trouble in paradise?"

"No."

"Where's your man?"

"Coming."

"Girl, that boy
is trouble
you don't need."

"What do I need,
Mary? What
do I need?"

"Hell if I know,
bitch.
I'm just trying
to be nice."

Nice, my ass:

I swear
she gets off
on getting up
and
leaving
me
alone with
my misery.

Cornered

When we go out,
we are not

Random Boy
        &
Forgotten Girl

anymore.

We are some kind of
four-legged organism.

He stands where I stand,
I sit when he sits,
and none of this is planned.
It's just
how we are
now.

If I laugh, he picks up
the vibrations in the
air and smiles.

Because of this
biological connection,
I feel my boy's muscles tense
before Peter X appears.

Peter X doesn't seem to see me.
His glare is connected to
Random Boy. "Can we talk?"

I open my mouth and close
it as Random Boy peels

his hand from mine like
a scab from a wound.

All three of us stand there,
gaping.

"Go to the tree house," Random Boy
whispers in my ear. He squeezes my
hand.

On eye contact with Peter X,
I know I should stay,
but I don't.

Peter X
doesn't argue.

My Un-proudest Moment

Picture it:
me, kneeling in muck,
digging my fingers into
moist moss to stay upright.

They didn't know,
(did they?)
I was there
watching
the few calm words
before
the thunderstorm
of punches
Random Boy threw.

I thought I'd seen him at his worst,
but what I saw
him do to Peter X
changes everything.

Or maybe it wasn't
so much what *he* did.

Maybe, the main thing
that kills me
about that moment
was me,
hiding,
unable to move,
silent as an assassin.

100% Bullshit Free

He is bigger than I am, yes,
but I draw from something
greater than physical
strength.

He tries to
level with me,
but he might as well
be speaking Chinese
'cause all I see
is a pile of words in her
penmanship.
All I see is
the possibility of this
nameless piece of shit
stealing
what belongs to me.

So I don't wait,
I don't listen
to his reasons.
I pound
harder than I need to, use
reserves of anger I've been
storing since childhood.

I give
it all
to him.

Something flies from his pocket,
explodes in bright light
as it hits the ground

searing the moment
in my memory.

What I'll never say out loud
is how it's her face
flashing in my mind
as my knuckles crash
into his bone and flesh.

How it's her I'm hitting
when I thrash him.

As he's hanging there,
lifeless as a worm,
I warn him:

"Don't speak
to her. Don't look
at her. Don't even
think of her, or I'll
finish you."

Tree House Rendezvous

From the old plywood platform, I hear
normal night sounds and smell
the evening rain ready to arrive.

I didn't have a choice, did I?

When he comes to me,
he smells like sweat
and blood. His
expression is
dazed,
I guess.

I run
my fingers
across his fuzzy scalp
and listen to the sorry
sobs he makes
into my lap.

I thought he'd be mad,
and I'm so confused,
but relieved
he's something else.

No matter what he shows
the world,
right now
he is totally
vulnerable,
a little boy
who just met
the biggest, baddest
wolf (the one
inside himself) and

somehow
survived.

The sobs
grow wilder
though quieter,
so I take off a layer—
remove his jacket and
peel away his shirt.
He presses against me,
lets me know
it's working, so I shed
my layers, too,
until
nothing is
between us. Soon,
he is my
big, strong Man
again.

He walks me home
afterward, the long way,
avoiding the blood-stained corner.

It is
just us,
and a thousand
stars. If only
the night
would not fade away
into light,
everything
could stay ignored
and okay.

When I Next See Peter X,

I understand
the stares,
the whispers.
I feel . . .

When I try to
talk to him, he
ignores me so
hard the veins
in his black and blue neck
strain
solid.

Should I
have stayed? I didn't
know he would . . .

(. . . maybe I did).

I didn't do it,
I didn't
bruise
his skin,
so why
do I feel
like I did?

I Try to Return the Phone to Peter X

but first, I carefully wipe dried blood from
the cracked screen and polish
it to a sheen.

(Mary slipped me the phone
on the sly
at the corner
one night
when Random Boy wasn't looking.)

I wait outside chem,
aware of everything and everyone
in the hall,
aware of the sweat
gleaming from my pores,
aware of every pixel
of his 182 digital shots
of me.

As he limps with dignity
I can't muster
toward me,
I am aware
this probably won't go well.

He spots the phone in my hand
and his eyes flicker and blink in
misunderstanding.

"Thanks."

"Thanks."

(Our silence seeps
past the lockers, attracting
an audience

he doesn't acknowledge
and I can't ignore.)

"So, I hear you still have a boyfriend."

I nod and swallow.

"That's . . ."
(This stretch of time, mere
nanoseconds,
I scroll through a million words
to finish his sentence:
typical, insane, stupid,
masochistic, true, psychotic . . .)
". . . enlightening."

Enlightening. I make a face that begs
for more information,
but he doesn't offer.

He just captures my confused face
on his microchip
and moves on.

Like Mother

When Dad left,
Mom stared at the door
that was closed on her
for hours.
Later, she explained
she wasn't ready to take
the first step
into
inevitable
ever after.

What finally
roused her
from the worst
dream (reality)
was me

rifling through
the spoiled food in the fridge.
While *she* was ready to starve
to death, she wouldn't
let her daughter
do it.

She got up
to make
macaroni and cheese
from a box
(baby steps)
that night.

Roundaboutly,
I saved her life,
and she taught me

a lesson
about how much I can take:
infinite amounts,
but,
when it comes to watching others hurt,
like my mother,
I rise from the lie-down-and-take-it
position
real quick.

Details

His eyes are
so familiar, I see his history
in the white,
his misery
in the blue.

I know him so well
that sometimes looking at his face
feels like staring at a mirror.

His hands
brush my skin
unaware,
but his kiss
senses something
awry.

"What is it?"

"I don't think we should—
I mean—"
(This is hard,
but I have to.)
"You & Me
is
over."

(The silence lasts longer
than our relationship.)

*"Because of that guy
who begged like a baby,
who you left
me to punish
for you?*

Don't pretend
like you didn't
know,
like you didn't
thank me
after."

(Is that what I did?)

That is not what I did.

"It's not him . . ."
(I make so much sense, I'm pretty sure I'm not
"It's me.
Your love,
though amazing,
feels too much like
pain. I can't take
the—"

"I promise—never again."

Promises.

"You can't."
I can.
"Please don't."
I do.

Break Up

So it's weird
how you think
you want something
for a thousand years,
but how
when you get it,
it sucks.

There

All I do is stare.
There are tangles
in my hair.
I don't care.
I go nowhere.

I can't bear
to share
the air.

It isn't fair.

Are you there?
I want to tear you
from my brain.
I want to be unaware.

Are you there?
Do you care?
Do you stare?

Do I Stare???!!!

Girl, I thrash.
I hurt.
I cut.
I use
booze and marijuana
ways to stop my mind
from flowing
in its natural
direction: to you.
You are unhealthy
for me
and all I want.
You are
the
nuclear bomb
that changed
everything
and then
vanished
into
a mushroom cloud.

What kills me
is how easily
you could take away
every ache—

You play
me with your stupid words
instead.

You are one beautiful demon.

Secret

I wish it didn't have to be this way.
Is there something you can say
to make me stay?
Then say it,
please.
I don't want to go.

13 Blocks

exactly—
from window to window,
door to door.
In 13 blocks,
19 minutes,
a right,
and a left,
I could be with you,
holding you,
even if
it's only for old-time's sake.

Between us
is a coffee shop,
a grocery store,
history, and
a snarl
of misunderstanding.

But when I think
of it as
13 blocks,
you don't seem
so far away.

Get Back

*She don't even
come to the corner
where I anticipate
her
like a freak.*

*I know she needs me
as I need her.
I know if I could get
her out of my mind
and into my arms,
she'd relent.*

*I don't know
who that beast was
that took me over,
my soul inheritance
from my father,
I suppose.*

*All those chicks
she hates
hate on me:*

"What'd you do to my girl—
that she don't come
down here anymore?"

*I ignore them
—invisible as the buzz
of tired, fluorescent lights.*

But Mary persists—

"She ain't
that kind of girl, you know?

She ain't the kind
you tap and forget—

She's my friend."

"Bitch, she is NOT
your friend.
You don't even
know her.
She don't even
like you
a little."

For once in her life,
Mary is silent.

"She's done with you,
isn't she?"

I smoke.

"Done with all of us, most likely?"

I nod.

"Shit. That seems
about right,
don't it?"

There,
now
Mary
understands.

"She was just
slumming with us,
huh?"

Private Caller

"Hello."

His voice in the receiver
strokes some string
in my heart before
I realize it's him
asking for
a reprieve—

*"You can change your mind
before the sun comes up,
but just for tonight,
pretend I am
as good as
you want me to be."*

"Do you promise
you can control . . .
. . . it?"

"If I hurt you, I'll shoot myself."

Something about the
black of night
makes everything feel
like a fantasy
that doesn't count
in real life.

I don't even look
before I leap
from my window
to the porch roof
to the wet evening
grass. I listen to the

rhythm of my sneakers
pounding pavement,
practically running
to phantom him.

I get so excited as I walk
to the tree house,
but I also wonder what I'm doing
and if I'll ever
go home
again.

This night's
first sight
is different
from each
previous
meeting,
because
we have
all those
forever
feelings,
but just
one night
to feel
them.

We are intensified.

For a couple hours
we hug
and talk
as if we hardly know
the worst parts
of each other.

We pretend
like All Those Things
never happened.

We kiss.

His hands are as soft as water,
rinsing away shared memories
across my skin,
chasing them out
into the night.

It feels so good,
like a warm bed
on a cold morning,

like a perfect song
I overplayed
and forgot existed.

And that makes it so much harder
when I see the first hint
of lazy pink sunlight in the sky,
to put my
pants on,
and end this
dream
again.

But that's the thing
about dreaming.

Eventually,
you have to
wake the hell up.

Gossip

Before he and I
spent all our days alone
together,
I used to spend them alone
by myself
with a book.

Now,
everywhere I go,
every book I open—

It's like I'm living, but
without an essential organ:
for instance, my heart.

In the light of day,
it's like
he's vanished.
All that's left of his ghost
is overheard conversations
about his supposed
goings-on.

Today, they say
he and Mary stayed at the corner
talking 'til 2, and then they
went out to the old tree house . . . and . . . and . . .

—I do the math—

That means he called me after
Mary & he
did
(Oh. My. God.)
it.

Why Her?

Man, it's always the girl
you let creep closest
to your heart
who stabs you
in it.

That's why I don't usually
allow chicks
proximity
to my soft spots.

Yet,
he picked the chick
who would hurt the most
to screw
me with.

"Why her?"

"I don't know. She was there."

(Silence)

*"I don't mean it like that. I mean I didn't mean to
the chick who would hurt you most."*

"And how could you call
me
right
after?"

*"Because.
Because . . .
Because—*

*Having her in my arms
was worse than being*

238

alone—just made it that much
clearer that I don't have you.

And I thought
I needed something,
but that
wasn't what I needed
at all.

I.
Need.
You."

Apology

*You know how I said
sex was sex
and
you
are special?*

That wasn't a lie.

*She and I
were nothing
but sex,
and drugs,
and rock
and roll—*

*late-night
wishes,
and tree house
dreams.*

*You
and I
are
forever.*

I Don't Know Why

I go to the corner
tonight. Mary is there
to confirm
my worst nightmare
with sideways stares
and guilty smiles.

Sigh.

Eventually
I get up the nerve
to ask her
if it's true.

"Did he sleep with you?"

And she tells me yes,
and how it wasn't
the best. She says,
"Girl, you don't know what you're missing,"
as if sex is as
interchangeable as
fast food. You got to
try 'em all
to really know what you like.

I don't know why
I ask her
for all
the sordid details.
I guess I'm like
those girls who cut,
except I like to
gash

my brain
with shards of reality.

That's how I
remind myself
I'm alive
and life has meaning.

She tells me how his
fingertips felt
on her back,
and I have a sort of
metaphorical heart attack.

I step back
from the conversation
and can't stop
watching her
descriptions
in my head.

"So you're a thing
now?" I ask.

And she laughs.

"I hope he thinks so."

She *laughs*.

"But girl, I was just
fooling around,
using him
for you.

Chicka, I was doing you a favor."

I Admit It

We fit, Boy, we do.

I want you more
than heaven,
more than that happiness I had
when I was a kid,

but I can't keep you
and respect myself.

Has Been

Girl,
this ain't poetry;
it's truth.

Always has been.

When you & me
are we,
we can
take this shitty world
right on. I can face the
assholery
(your word I love).

Now that you and me
are kaput,
I screw, I drink, I write
to escape—
I fight, too.
And even that
reminds me of
you.

You are everything.
Everyone else is disposable.
I am a mess.

Come back and make me right.

Even Mothers Make Sense Once in a While

The ground shakes as she vacuums.
Light erupts like lava when the curtains open.

Suddenly a divine spirit speaks
through my mother. (It's the only
plausible explanation.)

"I don't want
you to think
a man
can break a woman
because
this (points to her
self) was broken before
your dad
joined the picture.

And furthermore,
this (points
to herself
and then me) and this
can be fixed."

(I stare. My mother
has shocked me
before, yes, but
this time she does it
in a good way.)

She puts down her drink
(baby steps).

"I know I have been
—unavailable—
but a mother can tell

when her baby's heart
is broken."

She hugs me.

Through the gin and tonic breath,
and the years,
I smell
a tiny, faraway trace
of a closeness
we used to have—
a safety I forgot existed.

I resist for
a moment,
but then
my instinct
for
survival
kicks in.

I pull her in
and she lets me
cry. I babble
and bubble
and effervesce.

I sob
like a baby,
and grope
for
relief
in her
embrace.

Believe it or not, I find it.

Imagine a Chess Board

I can see
all the potential
moves.
I go over
the possibilities as
well as their consequences
hourly.

When I dream of
you grown up
and married
to a Random Chick
like me,
I kind of
want to puke,
but I can't let
my love for you
make decisions
for me.

As you know,
all I really got
is me—

Dedicated

Do you remember when we first met?
We're just two lost souls swimming in a fishbowl.
Nothing compares to you.
Tell me, baby, where did I go wrong?
For you I'd bleed myself dry.
We belong together.

You're just like me, only beautiful.
Forever, trust in who we are,
nothing else matters.

Reply

I do believe that I've had enough.

Do It Once, Twice, Right

Gone,
I say
and walk away.

Maybe if I think
hard enough
about not thinking,
try
as hard as
all get out,

I'll be forgiven,
and he'll be forgot.

Mixed

Hanging upside down
from my bed,
listening
to playlists
that chronicle
our entire
relationship.

They have titles like
First Stare and *Final Glare*.
I sit up,
take a swig
of gin and tonic,
and dwell.

I don't mean to be
a traitor to my generation,
but why
didn't I
listen to my mother?

Not what she said
(clearly, that's BS),
but what she whispered
through all that
wasted time,
those sad sorry
lines
I now recite on cue.

What are you going to do?

Your friends
were mine first. All you
got is a drunk mom
to keep
you
going on—

Date Night

Mom and I
decide
to get
dressed up
and go for Thai.

Then maybe a movie—
a romantic comedy.

"'Cause love is funny,"
I say as she applies
eyeliner.

"Exactly,"
she says with a laugh
almost
as sarcastic
as mine.

Thanks. For Nothing.

Just so you know
I will never feel the same
about anyone.

You ripped out my heart and
stomped on it, then
put it back, all broke the hell up.

You are a bitch.

The Line

I know you're not perfect.
Believe me, I know.
But I never felt that way, either,
and never will again.

I thought my dad leaving
was bad.

I thought my mom crumbling
sucked.

Don't worry.
From now on,
if I feel love happening,
I'll pull my heart back
into myself
and keep walking.

Because losing real love
is too close
to suicide.

Don't go beating
yourself up
on my account.
Don't go saying
no matter
how hard you try
nothing goes your way.

Boy,
we were
the Real Deal,
and I would've
followed you

to forever,
15 or not,
but you had to
bring your hands
into it.

I could've carried all your pain, and you,

but
you
hurt me
physically,
and that's where I draw the line.

I still love you, though, to be honest.

Can we be friends?

This is Why I Have Abandonment Issues

I'd rather erase you
from my life,
take a pill to
dissolve
every memory of you,

end you like you ended me.

Keep the pictures.
Keep the notebooks.
Keep your lies.

I don't want them.
And I don't want to be
your friend.

Piss off.

Later

I stare at rainbow words
trickling down the whiteboard:
letters that signify chemicals,
compounds,
formulas—
it's all chaos to me.

Peter X slides into the seat
next to me
and says nothing
as usual.

But after a moment,
I know—I feel—
he is watching me.
As a kind of confirmation, the artificial snap-
shot sound says he's taking
a picture.

He slides, or rather screeches, his desk
closer to mine, and we wait for the
image to appear.

I look like me not making
eye contact
with myself.
Even I can't tell what I'm thinking.

"You know,"

Peter X says,

"I can go back in time
through these pictures,
but I prefer to go forward."

Peter X goes to slide to
another picture, and
I get this urge
to touch him, to pull him
close and kiss
the scar above his eyebrow.

(Baby steps.)

I put my index finger next to his on the screen.
I stop him from sliding me away.

Random Boy's hold on my heart
is such
that even now
when we are broken in two,
I feel like I'm cheating.

I trace the long crack on the screen
dissecting my face into now and then.

"Sorry about
everything,"
I tell him,
"your phone
and your . . ."

"Still works,"
he says,

his finger
sliding me back and forth
across his screen.

"Still a million perfect
pictures yet to take."

I watch his lips
as he smiles.

"Thanks for trying to defend me,"
I say. "I'm sorry . . ."

"No thanks needed.
No apologies either."

"No?"

"No."

"Well, what then?"

"Just a promise."

I nod, urging him to explain.

"Swear to me
that no matter what happens,
no matter how hurt you get,
you'll still be
that serial killer writer,
that strong, beautiful chick
I was obsessed with
in high school. Promise me
you'll always go down swinging,
and that you'll get back up
with that smile that
could corrupt a saint."

He slides past my picture
finally,
and

the viewfinder slowly spirals open,
clear,
ready
for whatever
comes
next.

Acknowledgments

s to Carl and Jane for all the love and support a writer could want.

s to my mom and dad for filling my childhood with books
ve. Thanks to Pete, Mike, Pat, Cindy, and Natalie for all of
nversation and laughter. Thanks to Richard for taking me to
tores to browse.

s to Toni and Senior for watching Jane while I wrote a lot of
ook.

s to my editor, Nicole Frail, and everyone at Sky Pony Press for
ing in my book.

s to my super duper betas—Karen Amanda Hooper, Megan
de, and Natalie Bahm. I believe publication calls for another
Disney.

s to R. Mata and Laurie Devers for being early readers and for
awesome.

s to my agent, Lana Popovic, for having my back.

s to all my professors and classmates at UAF and SJU, and
of the very special teachers before that who went above and
d for me.

you all so much.